Little Owl's Night

Little Owl's Night

by Divya Srinivasan

SCHOLASTIC INC.

Little Owl was having a wonderful night.

He watched the funny possum family waddle along in a neat row.

Hedgehog sniffed around the mushroom patch.

Skunk was eating berries because he could find no snails.

By the river, beavers gnawed at trees.

Turtle hid in her shell as fireflies danced all around.

Little Owl visited his friend the raccoon.
As they sat in the clover, fog rolled in and
hovered just overhead.

Moths fluttered toward the moon.
Silver dust fell from their wings.

Little Owl wanted to follow, but it was time to head home.

On the way, Little Owl flew by Grumbly Cave.
Bear was inside, snoring up a storm.

"Wake up, Bear! Don't sleep all night!"
Little Owl sang. "I want to show you the moon!"

But the bear kept snoring, as usual.
Little Owl flew home to his tree, gazing at the sky.

He wondered if the bear had ever seen stars.

Little Owl sat on his branch.
How he loved the night forest!

Frog croaked softly.

Cricket chirped smartly.

Little Owl heard rustling at the foot of his tree. Fox had come to say hello.

It was late now. The bats were gliding home.
"Mama," Little Owl whispered, "tell me again
how night ends."

"The moon and stars fade to ghosts," Mama said.
"Spiderwebs turn to silver threads.
Dewdrops sparkle on leaves and grass like tiny
stars come down.

Moonflowers close and morning glories open.

The sky brightens from black to blue,

blue to red,

red to gold.

"The rooster crows. The crows caw.
And the day begins," said Mama.

But Little Owl did not hear.

He was fast asleep.

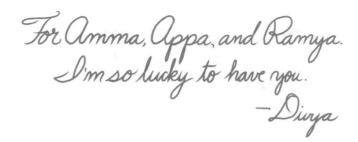

For Amma, Appa, and Ramya.
I'm so lucky to have you.
—Divya

ISBN 978-0-545-79070-3

12 11 10 9 8 7 6   15 16 17 18 19/0

Printed in the U.S.A.   40

First Scholastic printing, September 2014

Set in Sasoon Infant